The FIRST THANKSGIVING

By **JEAN CRAIGHEAD GEORGE**

Illustrated by **THOMAS LOCKER**

PAPER**S**TAR

The Putnam & Grosset Group

Library of Congress Cataloging-in-Publication Data

George, Jean Craighead.

The first Thanksgiving / by Jean Craighead George; illustrated by Thomas Locker.

p.   cm.   Summary: Describes how the colonists aboard the *Mayflower* founded

New Plymouth and celebrated their first harvest with a feast of thanksgiving.

1. Thanksgiving Day—Juvenile literature. {1. Thanksgiving Day.

2. Pilgrims (New Plymouth Colony) 3. Massachusetts—History—

New Plymouth, 1620–1691.}   I. Locker, Thomas, date,   ill.   II. Title.

GT4975.G47   1993   394.2'683—dc20   91-46643 AC

ISBN 0-698-11392-6

1 3 5 7 9 10 8 6 4 2

To Luke of the North.—J.C.G.

To Booch, Chris, and Gater.—T.L.

In a time so long ago that only the rocks remember, the last glacier began to melt. As it turned to water, mountains of gravel trapped in the ice were dumped on the coast of New England. One mass, shaped like a flexed arm, is Cape Cod.

On top of the gravel the glacier deposited huge boulders it had carried from distant places. One settled in Plymouth Harbor. It is a boulder of Dedham granite, the only Dedham granite in the entire area. A wandering pilgrim, it left its home in Africa two hundred million years ago, when the land was breaking up into continents. Eons later, battered by glaciers, all 200 tons of it came to rest in lonely splendor, on a sandy beach in a cove.

This boulder is Plymouth Rock.

The climate warmed. Wild grasses, flowers and trees took root in the land behind the huge rock. In time, their growing and dying made deep rich loam on which a magnificent forest grew. Into the forest came bear, deer, brightly colored birds, and the Pawtuxets, a tribe of the Wampanoag, The People of the Dawn.

The Pawtuxets planted corn, beans, squash and pumpkins. They hunted deer and turkey and fished the sea and the freshwater streams. Every year they gave thanks for these gifts to Mother Earth at the Green Corn Dance, which lasted many days.

In the early 1600s, Englishmen visited their shores more and more frequently. These men sailed in ships with butterfly wings, killed with guns, and kidnapped Wampanoag men for slaves. The Indians became deeply afraid of white men.

On a spring morning the Pawtuxets' worst fears were realized. A tall ship manned with armor-clad Englishmen sailed into their cove. The men came ashore and traded pots and beads for furs and fish. Then they tricked seventeen Pawtuxet men into coming onto their ship, pulled anchor, and sailed off with them.

One of the men was Squanto.

The Pawtuxets were taken to Spain to be sold into slavery. As it happened, Squanto was sold to an Englishman and taken to London. He lived in the household of a merchant ship owner. He sailed to Newfoundland, back to London, and finally home to New England.

As Squanto jubilantly strode toward his village in 1619, he suddenly slowed his stride. No children clambered over the big rock. No voices sounded. He pushed back the bushes and walked into his village. The homes they called *wetus* were skeletons. The corn fields had grown to weeds.

All his people were dead of a European plague.

In grief Squanto returned to the English sailing ship and was dropped off on the coast of Maine for the winter. The following spring he joined Massasoit, the sachem of one of the Wampanoag Indian communities.

In another world across the ocean, King James I of England ordered every citizen to join the Church of England or be hounded out of the realm.

The Puritans refused to obey. They believed they had the right to worship in their own manner. They were arrested, imprisoned, and some were hanged. Under cover of darkness, a group escaped to Holland. There they thought of themselves as religious wanderers, whom we now call "Pilgrims."

After twelve years of poverty in Holland, the Pilgrims decided to seek their fortune in the New World. Financed by merchant-adventurers, they loaded two sailing ships with food, seeds, and tools for building and farming. They also carried firearms and armor to protect themselves against the vicious animals and the people of the New World they called "savages."

After long delays for repairs, only one ship, the *Mayflower*, was fit to cross the ocean. On September 6, 1620, one hundred and two men, women and children and their furniture, cocks, hens, pigs, dogs and nine cats crowded aboard that small cargo ship. The growing season was over in the New World and winter was coming. Trusting in God and their own courage, the Pilgrims nevertheless set sail.

Hardly had the *Mayflower* moved into the open waters of the North Atlantic than the skies blackened. A storm whipped the ocean into tumultuous waves. The wooden ship rode up swells as high as mountains and plunged into sea troughs as deep as canyons. Her timbers moaned and her rigging shrieked. No sooner did that tempest end than another rode in. Crowded below deck, the Pilgrims suffered seasickness. The children clung to each other and to their parents to keep from being thrown against the hull.

They prayed, sang, and read their Bibles without complaint. And they endured.

"Land ho!"

At seven o'clock in the morning of November the ninth, Cape Cod was sighted in the steely dawn. The nightmare, it seemed, was over.

Wishing to go no farther on the angry ocean, the Pilgrims agreed that New England, not the Hudson River shores, would be their new home. The captain sailed the *Mayflower* into the shelter of what is now Provincetown Harbor.

After scouting Cape Cod for a settlement site to no avail, they entered Plymouth Harbor where the pilot, on an earlier trip, had seen the deserted Pawtuxet village.

A landing party set sail for shore in December's freezing rain. Near an island the wind snapped the boat's mast and broke the rudder. The shallop was swirled out to sea on a raging current. A seaman grabbed an oar and, straining with all his strength, pulled the boat to shore and mended it.

On December 11, 1620, the Pilgrim men landed on Plymouth Harbor beach, jumped into the icy waves and, fighting the sea and wind, secured the shallop to Plymouth Harbor's glacial rock. Their clothes had frozen into boards by the time they lit a blazing fire in the deserted village. They warmed themselves, drank the sweet water of the springs that ran into Town Creek, and planned the village of Plymouth. The houses would be close together and near the fields already cleared by the Indians. On the top of the highest hill they would erect the platform or fort.

The Pilgrims had a home.

Building was delayed by a violent storm, and it was not until January 2 that trees were felled and sawed into boards. In less than a week the Common House was erected. Then in snow and wind, the men began hammering their own homes together.

Winter struck with such cruel intensity that Governor John Carver permitted the families to stay on the *Mayflower*. The ship would not return to England until spring.

Food supplies dwindled. The Pilgrim men killed a few fowl and dug clams and mussels. But they were townspeople, they knew little about hunting and fishing. As they grew weak, they huddled on the *Mayflower* in blankets and layers and layers of clothes. They sang and read the Bible. Governor Carver meted out five kernels of Indian corn to each person once a day. The scouts had found the corn stored in reed baskets buried in the sand of Cape Cod.

Disease followed hunger, and death followed disease. Eight Pilgrims died in January, seventeen in February, and thirteen in March.

The dead were buried in the darkness of night. The Pilgrims did not want the "savages" to know how many had died for fear of attack.

They marked the graves only with prayer.

When spring arrived, only fifty-seven Pilgrims and half the crew had survived. Seventeen were children.

Saddened but determined, the Pilgrims returned to their dank homes.

On March seventeenth they planted. The women seeded English herbs and vegetables in their kitchen gardens. The men planted peas, wheat, and barley. They split wood, sawed boards, gathered thatch-reeds from the marshes, and scouted for Indians. Although their military men and Commander Miles Standish had been shot at by Indians on Cape Cod, the Pilgrims had yet to meet one "terrible savage." The "terrible savages," for their part, were watching the Pilgrims from behind trees and bushes, learning everything they could about the settlers.

On a cool April day, hungry and thin, their clothes threadbare, the citizens of Plymouth watched the *Mayflower* set sail for England.

Not one person asked to return.

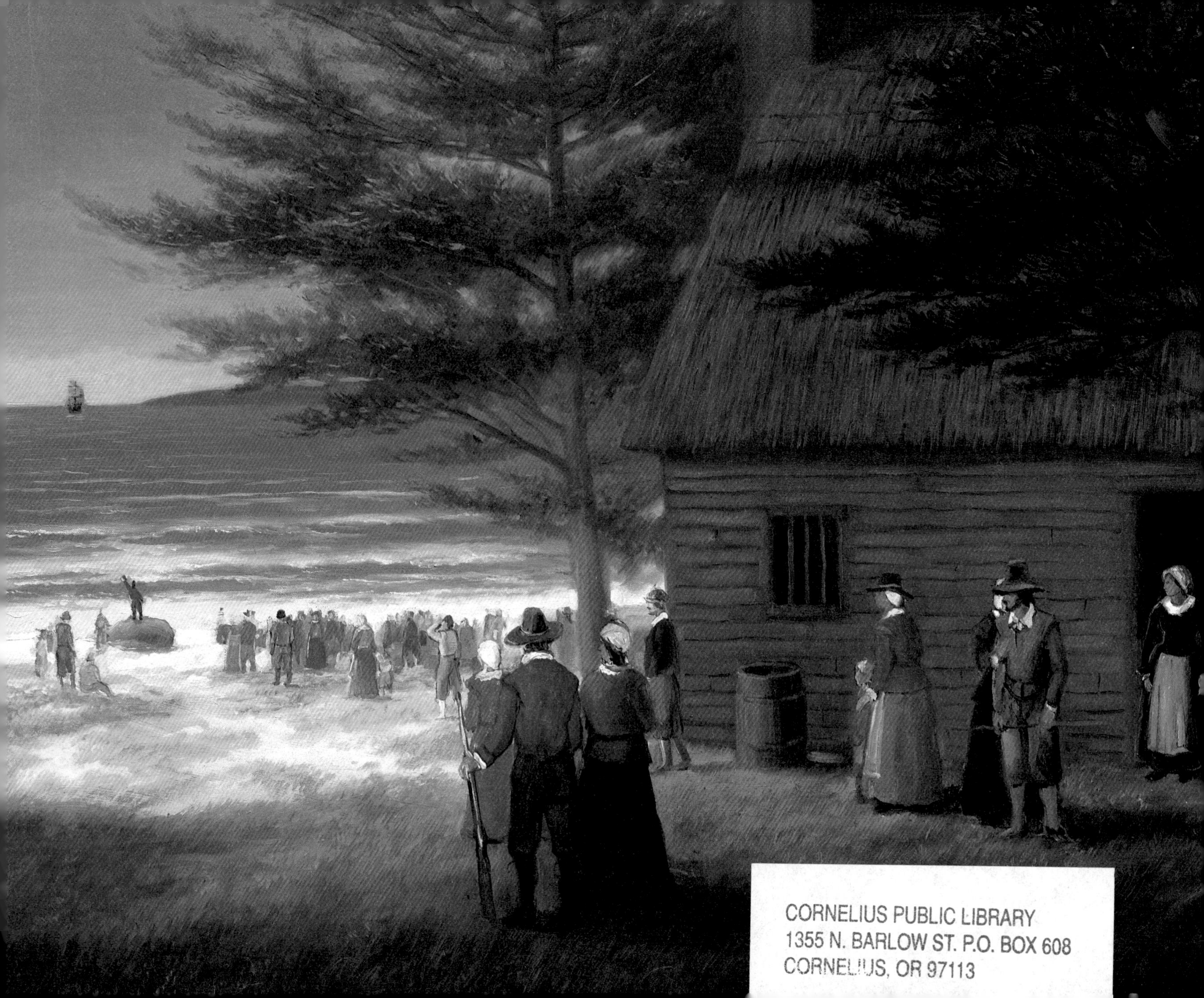

When the birds were trilling and the leaves were swelling, an Indian came striding into Plymouth. Tall, almost naked, and very handsome, he raised his hand in friendship.

"Welcome, Englishmen," said Samoset, Massasoit's ambassador. The Pilgrims murmured in astonishment. The "savage" spoke English. He was friendly and dignified. They greeted him warmly, but cautiously.

Samoset departed and returned a week later with Massasoit and Squanto.

For the next few days, in a house still under construction, Squanto interpreted while Governor Carver and Massasoit worded a peace treaty that would last more than fifty years.

After the agreement, Massasoit went back to his home in Rhode Island, but Squanto stayed on at Plymouth.

The wandering Pawtuxet had at last come home.

Squanto had seen that the Pilgrims did not know how to survive in the New World. They could barely catch enough fish for their colony, so he set out to teach them. Leading several men to the river, he waded into the water and feeling with his feet snatched a hibernating eel from the mud.

He showed the Pilgrims where the herring ran in spring and taught them to fish with weirs and nets. He also took them to waters where cod and salmon were abundant.

In late May, when the oak leaves were as big as his thumb, he led the men into a field and demonstrated how to grow corn. Squanto dropped several herring in holes, covered them with soil, and pressed four or five corn kernels into the soil. He planted beans beside the corn so they could climb the corn stalks. He planted pumpkins and squash between the corn rows. These were plants of the New World that grew with vigor in the rich land. Squanto shared with the Pilgrims the seeds that the descendants of his ancient ancestors had brought to New England from lands as far away as Mexico and Peru.

When the crops were thriving, Squanto took the men to the open forests where the turkey dwelled. He pointed out the nuts, seeds, and insects that the iridescent birds fed upon.

He showed them the leaf nests of the squirrels and the hideouts of the skunks and raccoons. Walking silently along bear trails, he took them to the blueberry patches.

He told them that deer moved about at sundown and sunrise. He took them inland to valleys where the deer congregated in winter and were easy to harvest. He walked the Pilgrims freely over the land.

To Squanto, as to all Native Americans, the land did not belong to the people, people belonged to the land.

He took the children into the meadows to pick wild strawberries. He showed them how to dig up the sweet roots of the wild Jerusalem artichoke. In mid-summer he led them to cranberry bogs and gooseberry patches. Together they gathered chestnuts, hickory nuts, walnuts, and hazelnuts in September.

He paddled the boys into the harbor in his dugout canoe to set lobster pots made of reeds and sinew. While they waited to lift their pots, he taught them the creatures of the tidal pools.

The harvest of 1621 was bounteous beyond the most hope-filled dreams of the Pilgrims. Corn, beans, pumpkins, wheat and barley spilled from baskets. Larders were stacked with dried venison, salmon, herring, cod and duck. Racks of wild berries lay drying in the sun. The chickens laid eggs abundantly and the cats grew fat on field mice.

It was time to celebrate. The terrible winter was done. The suffering was past.

The new Governor, William Bradford, asked Squanto to invite Massasoit and a few friends to a feast. He sent men out to shoot turkeys and ducks. The women baked. Boards were set on barrels, covered with precious linens, and placed in the middle of Leyden Street, the only street of Plymouth.

Massasoit arrived the day of the feast with five deer and many turkeys. With him were not just a few guests, as expected, but ninety. For a moment the cooks were shocked. Then they recovered and quickly went to work. More bread was baked, more vegetables were cooked, more turkeys were stuffed with bread and cranberries.

For three days the Pilgrims and Indians feasted, played games, and shot guns and arrows. This was not a day of Pilgrim thanksgiving, which was every Thursday from dawn to dusk. This was pure celebration.

Neither the Pilgrims nor the Indians knew what they had begun. The Pilgrims called the celebration a Harvest Feast. The Indians thought of it as a Green Corn Dance. It was both and more than both. It was the first Thanksgiving.

In the years that followed, President George Washington issued the first national Thanksgiving proclamation, and President Abraham Lincoln proclaimed the last Thursday in November a holiday of "thanksgiving and praise." Today it is still a harvest festival and Green Corn Dance. Families feast with friends, give thanks and play games.

Plymouth Rock did not fare as well. It has been cut in half, moved twice, dropped, split and trimmed to fit its present-day portico. It is a mere memento of its once magnificent self.

Yet to Americans, Plymouth Rock is a symbol. It is larger than the mountains, wider than the prairies and stronger than all our rivers.

It is the rock on which our nation began.